Anonymous

Katie and other Poems

Anonymous

Katie and other Poems

ISBN/EAN: 9783337398163

Printed in Europe, USA, Canada, Australia, Japan

Cover: Foto ©Andreas Hilbeck / pixelio.de

More available books at **www.hansebooks.com**

KATIE

AND

OTHER POEMS.

LONDON:

WYMAN & SONS, 74-76, GREAT QUEEN STREET.

LINCOLN'S-INN FIELDS.

1885.

CONTENTS.

———◆◇◆———

PREFACE

If these poor husks of words do hold some grain
  (I know not whether :—the gladiator reads
  But ill the arena's varied chance ; he needs
All for each pass, nor, till his foe lie slain,
Can wait on thought), if these, I say again,
  Do hide but here and there some tiny seeds
  Of truth, welcome the hand the flail that speeds,
Scattering the husks : I have not writ in vain.
Oh critic, lift the lusty flail, my sheaf
  Threshing, till all the floor with husks be spread :
  The gentle wind will kiss them into bed
Beside the passing summer's mouldering leaf :
  But, if one grain thou find'st in all my store,
  Sow it, perchance that one may bring forth more.

Sept. 6th, 1885.

KATIE.

I.

O Summer day ! how pleasant 'tis to rest
  In flick'ring shadow, when the quiet land
Lies lapped in sunshine, and the ocean's breast
  Pants as its ripples touch the gleaming sand.
O Summer day ! how burn the wanderers' feet,
  Father, babe-burdened mother, little one,
Climbing the dusty road in the noonday heat,
  Throats parched, eyes aching in the pitiless sun.
O Peace and Rest ! how sweetly smiles the day
  On the still haven of a gladsome soul,
Where Care and Sorrow never find their way,
  Where Light and Shadow laugh in one blithe whole.
O Peace and Rest ! how doth your memory,
  When Sorrow dwells alone within the breast.

Ring through the riven soul in mockery—
  Agony, agony, thoughts of Peace and Rest !

———

ONE April day, long wandering from morn
Among the uplands of my native shire,
Where the great billows of the rounded downs
Sweep skywards, from a valley's quiet deeps.
To fall in cliffs, and break in rocky ruins
Upon the sandy level of the shore,
I chanced to miss my way.

                    A streamlet brawls
Along the vale its sinuous course, marked out
By ragged undergrowth, with here and there
A stunted oak ; so wandering until
Its waters find the sea. where sea and sky
Look through a fissure in the billowy bosom
Of the great downs.

                    Dotted with sails, the waves
Smiled through the gap, whose double precipice
Cuts the soft Heaven with its cruel lines.
Hard by. a gable and some chimney-stacks

Peeped from a bower of apple-blossom. Thick
And high a hedge of evergreen shut in
The spot from prying eyes, and in the hedge
A gate, and swinging on the gate, a boy
Of seven summers cried he was a king,
And bade the dancing maiden on the sward,
Who gave her yellow curls to kiss the breeze
And laughed the sky back from her eyes, admire
How he could ride that gate. With smile I passed,
And dispossessed the monarch of the gate,
And, at the trellised doorway of the house,
Learned from its mistress's lips my road, and took
From her a cup of milk courteously offered,
And rested on the seat outside the door
Ere I went onward. But my stay, tho' short,
Planted her image in my mind. Still young,
Fresh as the breeze of Spring, her slender form
Girt with a spotless apron, and her hair,
Drawn back from a smooth forehead, showed in places
Gray streaks on the golden ripples that did shed
Their shimmer o'er the brown. Her wond'rous eyes,—
Like the great gateways of an Angel's soul,

Who saw the sadness of this Earth, her filth,
Her sin, and mourned, but buried all his sorrow
Under the glory of the Christ to come,—
Wide opened, sorrowful, yet full of peace,
Shed starlight 'neath their lashes.

                    In after-days
I learned her story.

                    How that light was born
Out of a blackness deep as Eternal Death,
Let this brief History witness.

                    Katie Meade
(Such was her girlhood's name), the youngest child
And only daughter of the village miller,
And better loved than all the stalwart sons
Who bore his name, did grow amid her downs,
Like the slight harebell on their naked flanks,
A gracious wonder in her rugged home.
Child, she was like a fawn among the flock
Of shaggy goats ; and maiden grown, she bloomed
A lily where her kin were daffodils.
They were all blue-eyed, ruddy, flaxen haired,
Tall and large limbed, square shouldered, mighty voiced.

Deep chested like their sturdy sire ; but she,
As slight as they were big, her shapely head
Rich with brown locks, where lurked the sunbeams all
That ever touched them smiling through their ripples,
Shimmering in golden laughter round her head,
Her cheek like a wild rose-bud, and her eyes
Two wondrous wells of light.   Her smile was worth
Another maiden's laugh, but when her lips
Parted in merriment, a stream of music
Rippled from the rosy portals, till the air
Laughed melodies with her.

            And her father oft
Would shake his frosty head, perplexed to know
How the child could be aught of his, or hers—
That gray-eyed Irish lass, who plighted troth
To him in years long dead, and left her land
To bear his sons, then yielding him her last
Best gift, wearied of life, lay down to rest,
Sleeping her dreamless sleep, beneath the yews
Up in God's Acre.   So he loved the girl
More than the rest for her dead mother's sake ;

Then for her sweeter self, as leaf by leaf
The pretty bud of infancy unfolded
Into the gracious childhood ; till, at last,
The maiden touched on womanhood, and the man,
Grown old and gray, did smile through all his heart,
And all his heart did leap to his honest eyes
To see so fair a morn rise on his age.

So Katie lived and kept her father's house,
Mended her brothers' clothes, and when they wived
And flaxen-headed children came, did love
To play the nurse would clap her hands to see
Some brother with his clumsy tender arms
Fondling his infant, helpless as the babe,
And shamefaced as a girl that owns her love.
And all the neighbours loved the lass, for she
Did lighten many a burden with her touch
Within her little world, and many a cloud
Did smile with rainbow hope above its darkness
At her sweet bidding.   One by one, for her,
The village swains did break their honest hearts,
And told the sad down-sides their hopeless tale :
But never dared to whisper in her ear

Aught of the arrows from her innocent eyes
That pierced their breasts, and filled them with her light,
Till they saw, all, how inaccessible
For them the heights of her sweet maidenhood
Must ever be.   Even the Curate paused
Once and again, too often, at the door
Where the pink roses listened to the splash
Of the pulsing water-wheel   too often saw
The smile in those sweet eyes—too often heard
Her voice's music—heard, and felt his heart
Tremble, as trembled in the dam beneath,
Mill, sky, and flickering play of gold and green
Shaken from overhanging trees.   Poor soul !
He took his pale-blue eyes and paler sermons
Out of the parish, one fair day in June,
And never came again.
                    So, peacefully,
Did pass her childhood and her youth, until
Her nineteenth year was drawing to its close,
And never breath of love had stirred her heart ;
For none of all her lovers spoke of love,
Not even the Curate.   Only once, indeed,

He sat for one whole hour in the long low parlour
Above the stream, and with the ceaseless plash
And busy thumping of the water-wheel
That shook the room, mingled his gentle tones
In slumberous discourse of Bible loves ;
What was the love of Eden—how twice seven years
Of service were as naught to all the love
That Jacob bore to Rachel—how the two,
Aquila and Priscilla, ever were
Associate in the Scriptures.   But the girl,
Naught witting of the trouble of his breast,
Did look on him with great unconscious eyes,
That his shy lips could never speak his pain ;
She could not read his eyes, so childlike she,
And, all unwitting of her beauteous self,
She dreamed not she was loved, not knowing Love.

   Nor knew, till tall Hugh Medwin crossed her path,
Dark Hugh, of stately form and ample brow,
And chestnut curls and eyes of fathomless night.
And Hugh did beckon, and the maiden's soul
Flowed from the channel of her quiet life
Into his turgid stream.   He asked her hand

Of the old miller : but the miller's words,

Few, yet with measured courtliness of mien

Spoken, did yield him answer, " My daughter, sir,

Has yet no thought of wedlock."   To him, Hugh,

" How know you ? have you proved her if she love ?

I trow she may, and if she do, the path

To thought of wedlock is but short."   But he,

The father, " Nay, I have not proved : but this

I know full well, my lass will never wed

Where I will not."   Then Hugh, " But your consent

Is all I ask.   I love the girl, and hope

She doth not mislike me."   And then the miller,

Hastily, " My consent she shall not have.

She is a child, too young to marry.   No,

Let her bide yet at home and mind the house ;

There's time for courtship and for marriage too,

And childbearing, enow, so let her be—

She is a babe, I tell thee."

                But not thus

Would Hugh be answered, and with kindling eye

And quickened speech pressing him, " I can wait

Her age to marry, yet I scarce can think

That nineteen summers pass upon a girl
And leave her still unripe for love and marriage.
But I can wait thy pleasure, friend, and hers,
Aye, I can wait, so I may gain her love
And, with it, thy consent."

      " Nay," quoth the father,
His stately form erect, while swift the blood
With heat the maiden whiteness of his brow
Did underflow. and sharply rang his voice,
" Nay, lad, I tell thee, nay ; and did'st thou ask
A score of times upon thy knees, my lass
Should not be thine, Hugh Medwin; if wed she will,
She'll choose among her likes, nor wed with one
Who deems himself her better——"

       " Her better ?
Never her better—I her better !—No ;
Her worse, a hundred, yea, a thousandfold.
She is an Angel out of Heaven."

        " Aye,"
The miller made reply, " an angel, she,
And thou would'st bid me give, to warm thy nest,
My angel ? Nay, man, be not hot, I have naught

Against thee ; but I mind thy father well,
I mind the Medwins all—proud, proud, all proud ;
And my white miller's coat would spoil the sheen
Of their fresh broadcloth. Dost not know that angels,
Too proud, did lose their first estate? and I
Would keep my angel, from such angels, safe.
Nay, lad, it cannot be ; my pretty bird
Must sing on other trees than thine."

And Hugh
Turned wrathful from the mill, and homewards ran,
And, hot with love and wrath, wrote, " Little Kate,
Thy sire will none of me ; he fears thy whiteness
Be darkened by the shadow of my life.
But I am thine, and thou, I trow, art mine,
And I do know that darkness is a lie,
And light is truth and truth must conquer, Love,
And thou wilt win my darkness to the light ;
And I am thine, and I will have thee mine,
Spite of all fathers—for I read thine eyes,
And I will have thee."

And Katie learned how love
Is bliss and grief ; and so one Summer's eve,

When the pale evening star was peeping from
The rosy glory of the dying day,
And all the sweets the Sun had given the Earth
Were stealing forth to tell the night how sweet
The day had been, he met her near the church.
He pressed his love, she yielded, and the twain
Did plight sweet troth beneath the climbing night ;
And one, returning from his upland field,
In the soft twilight, saw the lovers stand
Hand-clasped beside her mother's grave.

                          And then,
As days did wear, the miller, all unwitting
Of cause, felt something broken from his life,
Somewhat of sunlight that was wont to dance
About his path, till all his day was full
Of merry, twinkling eyes. The world was gray—
There was some cloud in Heaven, some mist on Earth,
Some chill upon his heart. And listening, he
Did miss the warbling laugh, the carol missed
That chimed to the ground-bass of the water-wheel
In rise and cadence, as the creamy foam
Churned by the wheel did froth above the green

Of the trembling mill-dam.   Roused at last to look,

He marked his daughter's face, and saw its light

Had faded, knew her erst so songful life

Had lost its song, and often in her eyes

He read of tears.   For, though she'd given her heart,

She would not, could not yield her hand until

Her father spake assent.   So in her breast

Was ever war 'twixt two strong loves, that made

Care in her youthful heart and smileless eye,

And lip without its laugh.

               Her father, sad

To see the change, and wrath with himself to know

The change had been so long without his seeing,

Did press the maiden, and did learn the cause ;

And then flamed up in sudden fire of speech,

Calling it rank rebellion, want of love

To a kind parent, and other of the like

In many words, until the child did rise

And throw her arms about her father's neck,

And nestled her bright head in his gray beard,

Cooing between her sobs—" My dear, my dear,

I will not grieve thee.   Nay, my love, I know

No will but thine, and I will never wed
If thou will not—but love I must, for love
Is not of will : and two do hold my heart,
And so I will not wed, but I will die,
And will not grieve thee, father.

                    Nay, frown not,
My heart is small, too small for two great loves
To struggle in, and they must be at peace
Or I shall die, and die I will my dear
For thee—and Hugh."

                 And then her sire, whose wrath
Was weakened by his mighty flow of words,
Did draw her to him, and did kiss the tears
From her sweet eyes into his own, yet spake
No word—but child and father knew right well
The child had won.

               So she did find her song,
And ere the winter came they twain were wed,
And the crisp air was merry with the peal
That shook the little belfry on the hill
Through the brief autumn day.

               They twain were wed.

And Katie went to the farm above the valley,
Where all the Medwins, many hundred years,
Had lived and died, and handed down their lands
From father to son, till the old house was full
Of family traditions, and the old garden,
Wild as the passionate nature of its lords,
Rich as their fancy, girt the dwelling round
With living histories.   Her husband's love
Made of the solemn place a Paradise,
Where all the birds were nightingales, the flowers
Lilies and roses, and the common air
Æther of Heaven, for in those haughty eyes
She read the deeps of his strong soul, and knew
His was no common love.   The brow that wore
Naught but disdain for others wreathed the sun
About its temples when he looked at her,
And all his pride was melted in her love ;
So that his face grew tender as a woman's
Turned towards her, and playful as a child's
His mien with her, and all his strength was bent
To bear her burdens as her willing slave,
That she might walk the lighter.   Never mother

Was gentle as this man, no youthful wife,
Soft cooing to her cradled infant, breathed
Ever such melody as the liquid notes
That told his love in every common word
He spake to her, so that the girl did lean
Upon his breast and nestled to his side
As to a mother's, and did find in him
A child for all her childish moods; and yet
So strong, she shrank within his arms as in
A fortress inexpugnable did aught
Trouble her bosom, for he seemed to her
A great Archangel, from whose lightning sword
Mortals did shrink dismayed.

                    His was a stock
Of yeomen, prosperous in his grandsire's days
And earlier, proud, even in prosperity;
But when the times grew harder through the pressure
Of competition with the outward world,
Brought to their doors by the power of steam, and men
Who never paid the country's taxes, who
Yielded her no allegiance, and whose sons,
Whose fathers never worked or bled for her,

Jostled her children in the crowded marts,
And drew the money that should buy their food
Into the treasuries of foreign states,
And slowly, close by close, the fertile lands
Washed by the trout-stream in the valley passed
To strangers and to upstarts—then did pride
Strike deeper root, now in these struggling years,
Into the yeoman's heart, than it had held
When many a broad ancestral acre smiled
Around his home. And as the sire the son.
He could not brook that village boors and hinds
Should make themselves his equal, should bemoan
His house's broken fortune, or with laugh
Point to its fallen pride. Thus year by year,
As he grew poorer, so he drew apart
Further from others, till at last he dwelt
Within the shrunken limits of his farm,
With scarce a friend.

        And now sweet Katie came
To bid his pride unbend, to let his heart
Open to all the kindly influences
Of love, so that the man. leaving his pride,

Worshipped himself and his ancestral dead
No longer, casting all his heart and being
At her slight feet, till from such worship sprang
A love that rose to higher worship still,
Seeing her but the Angel of a Love
That wrought such love for him.

                    And men did say,
Seeing Hugh Medwin soften in his ways,
That he was either mad or like to die
(For so is human charity for those
Who seek the upward path); as soon would they
Seek Lucifer among the Seraphs' choir,
Chanting the praises of the Christ he nailed
Upon the Cross, as grant to proud Hugh Medwin
Aught of the grace of life.

                 So Kate and Hugh
Lived, loved, and saw sweet issue of their love :
And when the husband saw his babe asleep
Beside the mother weary with the birth,
Joy bent his pride, and, kneeling down, he prayed
For this new scion of a failing stock,
His tears dashing the radiant face, upturned

To his with half-closed eyes, where smiles did sparkle
Through drops that overflowed the drooping lashes,
Slow trickling down her cheeks, sweet drops of bliss,
Drops of the river of Life, the stream of Love—
   One day, one blissful day, for saddened thought
To strain back after, when the day was fled
And present darkness drove the wearied heart
Into its narrow chamber.
                One short year,
Winter and Springtide, Summer, Autumn, all
Sweeter than ever Seasons were before,
Dead !
      Oh the tearless, sleepless pain that gnaws
The heart of him who knows no hope, whose life
Lies like some quiet star, above his world
Distance incalculable, while his veins
Throb out the pulses of a mere existence,
Denying death to lull his grief to sleep.

II.

Sweet Katie, on a warm September day,
Did keep impatient watch beside the gate

When all was quiet in the house. Her babe
Slept since an hour or more his noonday sleep,
Hens, ducks, and geese, and all the feathered flock
Were fed, the morning's work was done, and all
Was still within the house—was still without,
Save when the quiet air was stirred by wings
Soft flapping in slumb'rous measure, as a dove,
Slow floating from its cot in the deep-eaved gable
Enshrined in creepers, like a white cloud, alit
Upon the sward, or thence returned —save, too,
The insect hum about the sunny walls,
Where hung the peaches asking to be plucked,
And under all the murmur of the stream,
The mill-wheel's drowsy voice, through the breathless air
Borne upward from the deep.   And Katie stood
Impatient, watching by her garden gate ;

  For yesternight, Hugh, riding to the town
To meet a kinsman, promised her that noon
Should not long wait his home coming.   To her
The little journey and the night from home,
His first, were matter of moment, and her mind
(More child's than woman's yet) waited his coming

Eagerly.   Something he'd bring, some trifle, such
A love-toy as may tell a wife that, wedding,
She did not lose her lover.   So she stands
Before the hour, and beats with impatient feet,
And shakes her head with pretty petulance
Not once or twice, when fancy leads her ear
Astray; then bends her neck, listening again,
Listening for horse-hoofs.   Ah! at last she hears—
No fancy now—faint, clearer, lost again,
Now louder, clattering madly down the hill.
" Nay, thus to ride so rough a path, my Hugh
Is mad or much in haste," she spake, and fixed
Her eyes upon the valley's farther side
Where the road wound in sight.   Nearer they came,
Those horse-hoofs, nearer in plunging gallop—shouts
Rose from the vale—swift flashing down the road
Riderless came the roan, sprang through the stream,
Breasted the stony path in full career,
Stopping at last before the garden gate,
Foam-flecked, trembling in every limb.

        She stood
With frighted eyes, and marked a streak of red

Upon his reeking neck ; marked too a leather,
Stirrupless hanging : marked without seeking, saw
Incuriously, yet paused to see, three sparrows,
Driven by the coming of the horse to leave
Their search among the dust, return—saw all,
All one in moment to her bruisèd sense,
Powerless to feel : then spread beseeching hands
To the little group of rustics gathered round,
In steadfast whisper through her ashen lips
Imploring help, help, help, and answering naught
To all their questioning.

          Men searched, nor traced
Aught of her husband. Till the light did pass,
They searched each mile along the road, and when
The morrow came they searched, but fruitlessly ;
At last, in a field hard by the road, they found
A halter hanging from an oak—beneath,
The grass was bruised and trampled, and the soil
Deep dented with the marks of horses' hoofs.
And on the seventh day they left their quest,
And, when the seventh eve did melt in night,
The miller came alone to the garden gate

Where she stood watching, as she stood all day,
From morn to evening all those seven days,
Waiting, waiting for tidings.   Speechless they looked
Each in the other's eye, the pale lips parted —
" My Hugh is not," she whispered, turned and went
Within the house and softly closed the door.

   And her great sorrow from beneath her heart
Loosed, in untimely birth, a second babe,
Her husband's last bequest.   But long they thought
The tiny casket held no spark of life,
And many a day after the wailing cry
First passed its lips, they feared from hour to hour
Lest the pale flame should flicker to a spark,
The spark fade into ashes ; but at last
The weakling burgeoned in a bud of hope,
And the sweet bud did open in a flower
Of healthy infancy.   The joyless wife,—
Who, day by day, like a machine, had done
The needful duties of her motherhood,
Tending her babe with all unconscious love,
Scarce marking if its life did wax or wane,
So frost bound all the waters of her heart

That erst had answered every breeze of joy
Or storm of trouble,— when the constant moan
That passed the fevered lips did cease, and when
The lines of pain did fade, and a pale smile
Did gleam along the little features, felt
That the slight smile did warm her icy breast,
And the dead waters, stirred to passionate storm,
Did overflow the channels of her eyes
In tears.   Sad solace for the stricken heart!
Yet solace still, for, as the storm did pass,
A wondrous calm possessed her soul, and Love
Spake to her yet again; did speak at first
Of the wee baby in her arm, and shed
A glow of tenderness through all her being,
For its poor little life : did murmur then—
But faint, at first, and fitful as a song
That floats from voiceless distance o'er the sea,
When the soft air doth breathe from its deep repose
Sighs that drop down upon the waves and die—
Of an eternal song of blended lives
In the To-come ; and daily, straining her ear
To listen for the song, she heard it swell

Into a quiet strain of hope.   So she
Looked onward, upward, listening seemed to hear
Among the rest the voice of him she loved
Singing of present being, in the land
Where he had gone before, singing of life
Passing unseen.   She thought she reached her hand
Through the dread shadow and did grasp his own,
Warm with the energies of being renewed.
Thus did Heaven draw her saddened, longing soul
Back to the pathway of her daily life,
Feeling that thus she trod the self-same road
With her dead Hugh   the road that climbed to God.
    So, as the days were gathered into weeks,
Weeks folded into months, months laid aside
Each in his niche in the temple of the Past,
Katie did grow in strength, and learned to smile,
Aye, and to laugh, and sport with her two babes,
And all the home-life sped its course again
With work for every season, as of yore :
And none might mark the one great blank that yawned
About the hearthstone.

                    The old miller came

More oft now Hugh was gone, and gladly saw
Brighter his child than he had thought could be,
Seeing her grief. Oft would he sit and nurse
The maiden babe. At times his memory
Looked backwards in his life, then kissing the child
He'd call her Katie, speak of his dead wife
As one that left him yesterday, and tell
The little one how dear she cost him, till
Sudden he'd mark his child, then smiling close
Perplexèd eyes, and shade them with his hand,
Bidding the Present wake. She, too, would sit,
While her boy played about her, with the babe
Close pressed unto her bosom, and would pour
Into unheeding ears its father's praise,
Seeming to soothe the hunger of her soul
Talking to one who had no speech of words,
Yet whose great eyes would look an answer, so
That she did feel some angel passed from Hugh
Into the infant's soul to bid her live.
Fain had she put a drag on the wheel of time,
Bringing the days of speech, and robbing her
Of this imagined converse with her dead,

And she would strain the babe, whose rosy finger
Sought for the tear that glittered in her eye,
Close to her sobbing breast, and rain her longing
Over the little face.

     Passed thus some years
Of widowhood, and they who knew her not
Deemed Hugh forgotten, but who read her ways
Knew well how every Sabbath morn she climbed
Up to the churchyard. One had seen her there,
Before the smile of morning lit the heavens,
When the gray dawn was creeping up the East
Among the paling stars, kneeling beside
The simple cross of stone, and, when the day
Had leaped full panoplied upon the world,
Did meet her home returning, and did mark
In the great eyes that saw him not how she
Did make of that small cross a Bethel, whence
A ladder rose to God, where angels passed,
Angels repassed the way from Heaven to earth,
Angels of comfort passing from His Heart,
Angels of prayer from her pure soul. No week,
But its first day saw smiling on the stone

Fresh-gathered flowers, wet with dew and tears,
Weaved round the beam.   Upon the cross was graven
In golden letters " Rest," and at the foot
Hugh's name and age, and underneath the words :
" He was not, for God took him."   When the babes
Were older grown, the three were often seen
Up in the holy acre. Thence the eye
Can follow all the windings of the vale
Down to its gates of cliff—can see the stream
Now flashing in the sunlight o'er its shallows,
Now passing into mysteries of shade,
Until it turns the flank of the great bluff
That hides its course, but still, beyond the bluff,
Splashes of silver in the distance tell
Where it laughs onward,--thence, too, one may see,
Over the down-waves' crest, the waves of ocean,
Shimmering golden at morning. or aglow
With noontide rays, or spread with a laugh of green
Where all the merry purple shadows race
Swift as the clouds, their parents, in the blue.

　　There Kate would sit, and muse, and drink the day
Into her soul, her children at her feet

Sporting, and often she would try to teach

The little minds to grasp a father's love.

Sitting beside the cross, she taught her boy

To point his little finger to the sky

And lisp out " Father," and older grown the child

Would lift his sister's chin in his chubby hand.

Guiding her eyes above, framing his lips

To speak the word, whose sense they had not learned

Nor ever fully knew.

           So happily,

If sadly, passed her days, and so had passed

For many a year in tranquil flow, had not

A busybody from a neighbouring town,

Itching to tell what he had best concealed,

Burst with a seething torrent of unclean rumour

Into her quiet stream.   Only a tale,

Such as another heard from a friend, who heard

Somewhat from one and somewhat from another,

And so on ; but a tale that could not rest

And be a tale alone.   It must be proved

Or truth or lie, for had it aught of truth

'Twould tear her cult of love out of its Heaven,

And shatter its temple.   And if it were lie,
Then let the lie be slain ; thus should her god
Dwell on his altar evermore, serene,
Immaculate.   So on this tale she wrought
With anxious, aching heart and mind that strove,
Unwearying in its weariness, to find
The clue : and when at last the long-sought truth
Broke on her soul—O God ! this light of truth
Was utter darkness in her life, so black
That all her horizon ended at the grave.
Even the children, shadowed by the wing
Of this dread terror, passed out of her life
Into a dream, where all her touch was numbed,
And the chilled senses answered not the call
Of every day's necessities.   This truth,
That flashed along her soul and left the night
Shivering behind it, told her this :

                              " Her Hugh
Lived not in Heaven, but in a felon's cell."

III.

Hugh did not die.

        That night, that pleasant night,
How blithe with chatter and carol of birds the trees,
Less blithe no whit the merry breeze that sang
Among their branches, blithe as the mellow laugh
The mill-dam's waters plashed to the sober thud
Of the busy wheel. How lovingly the sun,
Westering, looked his last across the vale
As Hugh splashed through the stream, and, lingering,
Turned yet upon his roan and waved good-night
To Katie standing by the garden gate.
Then down the valley, dim with the mystery
Of tender twilight creeping, creeping up
Hill-sides, whose crests yet blazed with golden light,
Passed with the day, and left his home above
In mellow sunlight, over the twilight world,
With his last smile yet lingering in his eyes,
With his wife's kiss yet warm upon his lips,
With his heart warm with love, and lit by hope,
And all the blissful tenderness which fills

A lover's soul when parted for a day
From her he loves, making a little shadow
In his sweet day of happiness.

      So rode

Till day did pass, till stars did peep, till night,
Hiding our planet, bade the universe
Look from the measureless void of space. So rode
Wrapped in his peaceful thoughts - the sounds that trembled
   trembled
Across the quiet night served but to help,
Not mar, the stillness — nothing, save the fall
Of horse-hoofs, rustle of leaves, when some soft breath
Came wandering through the darkness, a stray note
From a late waking bird. And thus his brain
Built airy temples, whose deep aisles were dim
With wonders. and whose fairy spires soared, soared,
Lost in a radiant mist of rainbow fancy –
Temples to one sweet deity, where he
Was priest, who daily, hourly, sacrificed
Upon her altar offerings of all
His mind might think of noble and of true :
For Love begat within his bosom thoughts

That dared to raise the ladder of Ambition
Upon his hearthstone. He had felt his strength.
And his new worship bade him stretch his arm
And climb for her, as he had never climbed
For self alone. Thus pondering, the road
Passed from the down-side, ere he marked the change,
Into a thick-grown wood, where twofold night
Clung to the deep arcades, where stars infrequent
Twinkled and flashed through the leafy tracery,
Where lingered yet the warmth of noon-day.

                                  Then
Men sprang forth from the night, his horse was thrown
Back on his haunches, and a sudden blow
Made sight and sense to cease.

                              He woke to life,
Nerveless and dazed, in a strange room, where all
Was sordid filth, where men and women spake
Worse filth than that which smeared the greasy walls ;
Where curses stood for prayers, and scowls for smiles ;
Where laughter was too horrible a thing
For speech, and made his spirit shiver ; where
All was of brute and naught of man. For days,

Restless, he tossed upon his filthy bed,
Till spite of all his health began to mend,
E'en though he saw that he was prisoner
In this foul cage.   But ere the second week
Did close, when yet too weak to stand alone,
He heard one night blows on the door beneath,
And whispers passed among the loathsome crew
That dwelt around him ; then, while the house-door
    cracked
And groaned beneath the unanswered summons, they
    fled,
Whither he knew not.   So he lay until
The door was forced, and he dragged from his bed,
To change his durance for a prison cell—
A prison—the dock a charge of robbery
Done on the spot and on the very night
When he was well-nigh murdered.   A remand,
And more remands, at last committed for trial :
And the evidence, the astounding evidence,—
His height, his hair and skin—nay, the very wound
Upon his forehead testified against him.
Traced by the officers of Justice, found

In a den of vilest crime with a bandaged head,
And the room telling of the very deed
Whereof he stood accused.   And thus the chain
Was woven link by link, and Hugh did stand
Astounded so to see his own misfortune
Bring him a felon's meed.   He had no witness,
His mouth was closed, even his lawyer scarce
Could hide a smile at his fond tale, but shook
His head and pursed his mouth, nor bade him hope
For credit with the jury.   Then did pride,
That could not brook to see his honest name
Dragged through the mire and branded deep with
      crime,
Rise in his heart, and bid him hide the truth
Even from Katie.   Better she thought him dead
Than knew him, like the scourings of the streets,
Alleys, and courts of London, swept away
Out of the ken of cleaner-minded men
Into the moral dunghills of the land—
The prisons.   Better far that she should deem
Him lost or murdered, than that men should point
The scornful finger at the felon's child,

The felon's wife, or friends should turn aside
Fearing to meet them, or immodest souls
Should force inquisitive pity on the hearts
That yearned for sympathy, or Pharisees
Should smile magnanimous welcome from the eyes
Cold with the self-sufficient righteousness
That filled their hearts and made their souls so light
That earth was far too gross for their holy tread,
So that they seemed to walk on air, thus far
They trod above their fellows,—worse meed than scorn
To gentle minds seared with affliction's brand.

So Hugh did hide his name, and would not taste
The wells of sympathy sweet Katie's love
Made to spring up within her breast. He knew
She would read truth in his simple story, would
Count it honour to soothe his pain and shed
Light on his darkness, and he should have known
That others' scorn or pity would not dim
Aught of the lustre of her Christ-like soul,
That all the sorrow of her heart would be
Only his sorrow and their sundered lives:
But impotent wrath so blinded him, and pride

So spurned the slander of his fame, that he
Could not or would not see the truth, and dreamed
He was a martyr for his wife, nor drank
Of her sweet springs of comfort, lest the source
Should be defiled and troubled by his taking.

    Nameless, he stood within the dock and marked
The smug-faced jury say the fatal word
That cut him from his name and citizenship,
And heard the sentence—ten long years of toil,
An outcast slave! Then judge and jury back
To wife and child and peaceful joys of home,
Without one thought for him for whom the grave
Closes on home and child and wife.

                  So Hugh
Passed from the world, and first it seemed that God
Would lift the darkened spirit into light
Out of the prison hospital. Ere long
The strength he'd gathered on his native downs
Shook off disease, and his poor riven soul,
Unwilling, felt its temple strong again
As erst in happy days. Better to die,
Than thus to spend his strength in slavery,

Not in the building of his home, to feel
All purpose fettered, all affections chained.
The stirring mind vacant of matter, alone
Feeding upon itself.

        Long years did pass, yet he
Marked not their passing, only knew the hour
That closed his daily labour, left him free
To plunge into his sorrow.   Oh! the nights,
The weary sleepless watches, like to his night
Of soul and being : better far the days
Of toil among his foul companions, where
Bodily slavery was the smallest ill,
Where every circumstance enslaved his mind
And bound it, as with fetters, till its wings
Drooped nerveless, till it lingered round its task,
His sordid task, his sordid daily life
Choked in the prison atmosphere, yet knew
No energy to soar into the Æther
Where all its longings pointed.   But the nights,
When the chained soul was freed, yet felt the chains
Still on its wings, and bruised and sore crept up
So far into the light that it could see

Its miserable shadow on the past.

Naught more—and yearned and yearned, and rent
    itself

In agony of longing for that past,—

The dead, lost past, so beautiful, so sweet,

So peaceful on its death-bed,—fearful hours,

When every pulse became a demon voice,

And the quick blood that filled his veins with fire

Seemed to stagnate within his bursting head

Until his brain was hell.

                  Oh! he had fain

Dashed out his seething brain against the wall

In his fierce madness, but that, when the force

That to the deed urged with resistless power,

Ever, 'twixt him and death, rose up the form

Of Katie, standing at the garden gate,

As he had seen her last, the westering sun

Looking his last across the vale, to rest

In smiles upon her head: and, with that vision

Cooling his burning eyeballs, the dread power

Would pass at once, and the strong man would sink

Shivering, in utter weakness, to the ground

Weeping, until from utter weariness
He slumbered till the morn.   Once he awoke,
When a short summer night did wane, and stars
Peeped paling through the guarded window.   Low,
Rising and falling through the quiet, came
The pulsing of a water-wheel, the plash
Of the stream falling o'er the weir.   His heart
Stood still in agony of longing.   There,
Beneath, he heard the sentry's measured tread
Turning upon his beat, and heard him once
Ground with a clang his weapon.   Still thud, thud,
Low came the wheel's soft song, the changeful plash
Of water   lower and lower- till all passed,
So that he knew not when.   Then slept ; a sleep
So sweet, that, when he woke, he thought that death
Had lifted him from Earth to Heaven.   Rising,
He scarce could do his work, so nerveless felt
His limbs, so dazed his brain.   But all did pass,
And the old horrors chained his soul.   One day,
When the long toil beneath the summer sun
Intolerable grew, even to him
Who cared so little for his body, when

The blood did surge, with every stroke he made,

About his brain, and all he saw was red,—

Sudden he felt a breath of cool sweet air,

And in a moment, on the arid ground,

He saw his wife, smiling with peaceful eyes

Into his own ; he heard the water-wheel

Merrily beating in the depths below,

Saw the broad shadow of the trees that stretched

Their arms about his home, and from their shade

Watched the hot labours of the harvest-field,

Heard the infrequent voices of the hinds,

Hoarse in the noon-day quiet   yet through all,

As in a dream, far on the extreme horizon,

Saw the blue-coated warder, heard his voice,

Chiding, bidding him work.   Then Katie moved,

Laughing, lifted her babe to him, he stretched

Glad arms to her with a wild rapturous cry,

And then a flash of orange-coloured light

Swept down and blotted all things from his eyes.

" Dead, no, not dead, but coming back to life ! "

This the first speech he heard, when many weeks

Had seen him tottering on the verge of death.

Opening his eyes, he looked, and saw a man
And woman talking near his bed. Then quick,
With sudden strength endowed, he raised himself,
As that sweet vision broke upon his soul,
" Where is she, where, my wife ! " and swept the ward
With hungry eyes : then falling back, " O Christ,
Dead, dead, aye dead, a vision of her death ! "
And lay in swoon for many an hour. But time
Rendered him feeble strength and raised him up.

   Then, too, he learned that he was free to go.
One of the men who stopped him on the road,
Taken and tried for murder, had confessed,
Before he died, the story of Hugh's wrong :
And, of her bounty, Justice pardoned him
For crimes he never wrought. This was the tale :
Hugh had been stopped, mistaken for another,
An agent homeward riding with the rents
Collected for a neighbouring squire. The thieves
Dared not leave Hugh unconscious on the road,
Willed not his death, although one of the three
Counselled to slay him. So they tied his horse
With a halter to a tree, and dragged him, bound,

A furlong, to their place of rendezvous,
A disused lime-kiln, where two others waited
With tilted cart, wherein they laid him down,
And bade them take him to the city. They
Waited till night grew gray to work their purpose,
But failed, and their leader earned a wounded head,
Sole pay for the double crime. They hid that day,
And the next evening passed, as best they might,
Back to the town and to their lair. But Hugh
Through all that night, unconsciously, did pass
Towards the city, and when morning broke
Was hidden in a wayside public-house,
The haunt of thieves and poachers, till the light
Did pass, and, ere a second day-break, came
To a filthy den in a dark London court,
A fortalice of human beasts. He knew
Nothing of all this journey, for his brain
Was injured by the blow, and many suns
Did rise and set upon the murky town
Before he saw the light. And, when the door
Of the foul stronghold was assailed, the gang
Fled by a secret trap in the cellar floor,

Leaving Hugh there to answer for their deeds,
Laughing, so said the man, to see their crimes
Fastened upon the guiltless.   He who led
The thieves was tall and large of limb, dark browed,
And, in the uncertain twilight, careless eyes,
Not noting features, might well see the man
And think him Hugh. The bandaged head completed
The lying identity.

    So Hugh was free.
Was free from chain and blame, and prison doors
Flew open at his word, and he went forth
Into the fresh free air.   But prison walls
Had pent his heart so long, those unseen chains
That bound his spirit had so worn his soul,
Chafing against them, and the growing years
Had riveted day by day fresh fetters, so
That all the heaped-up misery of his life
Weighed down his body and crushed low the flame
That warmed his being.   Broken in health and bent,
With step uncertain, and thin nervous hands
That closed and opened in a wandering way,
And the once stern unyielding lips, that spake

His strength of purpose, quivering at each word
That passed them, Hugh went out into the day
Taking the prison with him.   In his eyes
Such hunger, such ineffable longing dwelt,
As seemed would force his spirit from the clay
To fly before him.   Thus the dead was raised
Out of his grave, and, with his grave-clothes on
Rotting about him, and the earthy smell
Clinging for ever to him, bidden again
Live and give blessings to the light that made
His unaccustomed eyeballs ache.

                        So men
Do right the wrong they do.

                    Hugh heard the lark
Singing above him as they took him thence,
So free, so God-like in his liberty,
Soaring, soaring— oh, that he had those wings
To soar from Earth and learn the carols of Heaven
To teach him freedom !   And did the songster giv
New hope of life to him ?

                  Nay, rather poured
Discord upon his soul.   He heard the clank,

The ceaseless clank of those unloosened chains,
Within his bosom, dragged his fettered soul
Out of the prison clanking through the world,
Chained, till the Earth should open for his grave,
Chained, till the dust should lie about his skull.

IV.

Hugh did not write, he did not dare to write,
He did not dare to ask, lest he should learn
That, as he feared, the vision of his wife
Before he sickened did portend her death.
Unknown he left the prison, came by night
Back to his native village, wearily crept,
As dreaming, up the path that climbed the hill,
And stood, ere day did lighten in the East,
At his own garden gate. For one whole hour
He could not enter. Then, at last, he stole
Slowly along the path and raised the latch
(For never bolt or lock did close their doors,
These simple village folk), and groped his way
Into the well-remembered room, then struck
A match, and seeking hungrily around

Lit upon this and that of woman's gear,
Letters that bore her name, a hundred things
That said she lived, making his heart leap up
In gratitude. The blackness of the night
Was fading into morning's gray when Hugh
Stopped at his bridal chamber. Sick with joy,
Half fainting with the fluttering of his heart,
And all the agony of his struggling sense
Tearing his soul, he leaned against the wall
Ere he could turn the handle. Entering, saw,
When reeling sight could pierce the twilight gloom.
Only a bed with one still form, a pillow
Shaded with tresses loosened in her sleep,
Only an arm over the coverlet
Tossed, and a hand white little hand and thin.
With a gold circlet on the slender finger.
Only this in a darkened room, the face
Was hidden.—only this, yet strong to stir
A soul to storm and make the body tremble
Powerless. He staggered to the bed and fell
Down on his knees. She, stirring at the sound,
Did murmur something in her sleep. But he.

Weary and faint with the travail of his soul,
Passed into sleep kneeling beside her couch ;
And when his little maiden ope'd her eyes,
With pretty prattle welcoming the day,
And woke her mother with her cooing song,
And Katie saw her husband, who can tell
The secrets of her breast, that none may read,
Herself the least of all?   She crept from bed
Wondering naught, for, ever since the day
She knew he lived, knowing his deeps of love,
Felon or none, she felt through all her soul
He would return ; and through those weary days,
Not reckoning time, in madness of desire,
Making to be what could not be, did wait
To hear his footstep—waited, with a dread,
A horror, lest her Hugh should not be he
She dreamed him.

                    Oh, those days of waiting ! Oft,
When all the yearnings of her soul went out
In longing, she would look for him all day,
And wake for him the livelong night, afraid
Lest coming he should find her sleeping.   Hope

And fear were ever struggling in her breast :
Trusting and doubting, knowing naught, and tossed
Upon a troublous sea of thought, she longed for
Yet dreaded his home-coming—felt at times
That she must run and hide from him, nor dare
To see the face that crime had marred   then hated
Herself for doubting him, and yearned and yearned
To weep upon his breast, and bid him chide
Her want of faith.   For many months had passed
Since first the tale had reached her, and not yet
Aught had been heard of him.   Those months, so
    short
To others, had been centuries to her,
Had marked her brow with sorrow, and had struck
Joy from her eyes, and filled them with the fire
Of longing.
      And, when the woman saw his face
Lie pale and worn and sad unspeakably
Upon his hand, and marked his weary sleep,
She knelt beside him.   Even as she knelt
Her sense did leave her, as, with a wailing cry,
She clasped her arms about his neck, and he,

Waking, received the burden in his arms.

No words may paint those days of fathomless bliss,
When the two streams of life, long dyked and dammed
Apart, and gathered into stagnant pools,
Did burst their banks, and rushing through the cleft,
Flow into one again.

                   And summer passed,
And left the woods all radiant with the smile
He shed upon them ere he died.   Then came
The quiet days of autumn, when the rime
Glittered upon the red and golden wild,
Or the clear air was merry with the breeze
Sprinkling the ocean's breast with curls of white,
Till autumn faded, and downwards from the pole,
Killing the year by days, cold winter crept,
And nights were long and fog drew from the sea,
Wrapping the down-sides in its chilling mantle.
And the red leaves did drop beneath the rain,
And all was mournful in the narrow world
Around.   Then Katie marked her husband grow
Weaker and weaker as the days slipped by ;
For first he straightened like a tough yew bow

Long bent, when the string is loosed, and Katie
   joyed
To see some colour in his careworn cheek,
Some sparkle in the saddened eye, some tinge
Of his old self.   And in those autumn days
He learned to know his children.   But the boy
Was shy, and long time did not trust his father.
Like Hugh, the child could not love ere he knew :
Like Hugh in eyes, in shape, in ample brow,
But fair, like Katie, with her gold-brown hair ;
Like Hugh in all the powers of his mind,
His strength of will and purpose, like him too
In the shy soul, that drew itself apart
Into its inner sanctuary, nor brooked
Inquiry of those who had no right : withal,
Gentler than Hugh and blither.   When he learned
To know his father, then he gave his love
With all the passionate earnestness of his being,
As if the days to come were far too short
For all the lost love of the former years,
When his father was not.   And the little maid,
From the first moment that her wondering eyes

Lit on his weary face, gave him her heart
As erst her mother hers.   How sweet those days
Of mellow autumn sunshine, when their home
Was waking with a second songful spring,
And all the misery of the bygone days
Served but to foil the beauty of their Now.
But when the hand of winter held the earth
In icy grip, the joy did wane, for Hugh
Shrank at the touch of cold, and seemed to pine
And fade as summer flowers that feel the touch
Of a late frost.   Christmas was scarcely past
Ere he began to fail, and day by day
Thenceforward weaker grew.   His soul was free
And joyous as the breath of spring—so free,
The body, long pent within prison walls,
Dragged wearily behind the spirit's flight,
So wearily he heard the fetters clank
Upon his limbs.   The mind, so long imprisoned,
Had bound the body ; now, when the soul uprose
In strength and freedom, lo ! the dungeon bonds
Tied its frail temple to the earth.   So passed
The winter till the spring smiled out again.

And the brook tinkled with a merry song
Between its mossy banks, whence starry eyes
Of primroses did peep, and laughed to see
The steadfast sky above them, and below
The melting heaven in the dancing stream.

 Hugh sat one morning in his elbow chair
Before the open window, for the day
Was sweet with sunshine. It was an April morn,
The day when angels lift the cross of Christ,
Bright with the glory of the sacred burden
It bore of yore, risen, yet ever on earth
Searching the foulest spots with His pure ray,
Over a world, dark with the scowl of sin,
To tell men's souls that from the travail of death,
Of crime and sorrow, springs the white-robed soul
Into eternal life; even as the tree
That bore of old that awful fruit of sin,
A murdered Christ, gave to the skies a Christ
Starred with the myriad lights of deathless Love.
Across the valley, from the hill-side church,
Came the glad voices of the Easter bells,
Came from below the murmur of the stream,

Came from the trees the twitter of the birds,
Came from the sky the carol of the lark,
And with them all the prattle of his child
Mingled, until his spirit stooped and drank
Of the stream of peaceful life that flowed around.
Then little Katie climbed upon his knee,
And nestling to his breast, against his face
Laid her soft cheek, and cooed a baby hymn
Of Jesus and the children, till his sense
Passed into slumber, and the child lay still
Herself half-slumbering, murmuring now and then
Snatches of melody.   Then her mother came
Into the room to take her, but the child
Raised earnest eyes, and, with a rosy finger
Touching her parted lips bade silence, for
Her father slept.

              Yea, slept on earth, but waked
In Paradise, among the broken hearts
Healed with the balm of Love, and, like the child,
Nestling warm in a Father's bosom.

                    Thus
Hugh Medwin kept his Easter feast, and thus,

When the first darkness of the hour was gone,
Sweet Katie learned to look from sorrow here
Into the gladness of the Home, where Hugh
Was waiting for the children and for her.

SONNETS FOR THE CHURCH'S YEAR.

———◇◇———

ADVENT.

Lord Jesu come! The caves of storm unbind
  Their winter monsters, till the darkened main
  Breaks into madness, till hail, sleet, and rain
Drive down the shuddering pathway of the wind—
Thou art not in the tempest. Loud behind
  The forkèd terror that splits the night in twain
  Crashes the riven thundercloud's refrain—
But thunder echoes not Thy gentle mind.
Warm by my fire I sit, the tempest hear
  Surging around me, and my soul is wrought
  Into a surging storm of 'wildered thought,
Till all my being waits at my listening ear—
    Still! thou vain dreamer, quit the world of
      sense,
    Christ cometh in the voice of conscience.

CHRISTMAS.

SCATTER thy snows o'er all the northern land,
  Winter, and veil the earth with purity ;
Her miry foulness with thy cleansing hand
  Touch, and the foul before the pure shall flee.
Shine out, thou white Christ-Child, ere yet the
      sand
  Of the fast dying year is run, that we
May see Thy purity, and, with the band
  Of all Thy clean ones, cleansèd be by Thee.
Oh dear Babe Jesu, born at winter-tide,
  With storms and snows, if need, make clean my
      heart,
  Even as winter tempests bear their part
To cleanse the soilèd earth.   So at my side
  Come stand, thou white Christ-Child, in lowly
      state,
  Teaching me lowliness alone is great.

EPIPHANY.

Oh star, who led'st those Eastern kings to find
  The Blossom sprung from Jesse's withered
    rod,
  The wonder of their dimly-imagined God
Whispered of angels to each awestruck mind,
Look down from Heaven, give eyesight to the
    blind.
  May we, like those of old, with wisdom shod,
  Crossing life's desert in the steps they trod,
Seek Purity in Lowliness enshrined !
  Oh Light of Love, in whose pure ray abide
All Christ - like souls, our morning star Thou
    art ;
  Draw us to worship at the cradle-side
Where weakness claims the homage of the heart,
  For every white-souled babe is born to be
  To love-lit lives a new Epiphany.

PALM SUNDAY.

Hosanna !   Cast the offerings of the spring
  Under His feet, your voices raise on high.
Hosanna !   Till the sacred precincts ring,
  And distant Olivet takes up the cry.
Hosanna !   On the ground your garments fling ;
  Shout, little voices, shake the steadfast sky.
Hosanna !   Babes, smile praises to your King,
  He Who bade children come to Him rides by.
Forbid them not.   The children sing their lays
  Over the ripples of the crystal sea.
Forbid them not.   Christ Jesus loves their
    praise,
  And smiles to see them laughing in their
    glee.
Shall *we* forbid them then on earth ?   Oh, nay !
Sweet Jesus rides where children laugh and play.

GOOD FRIDAY.

Oh wonder! Heaven's high city wrapped in
    gloom,
  And all the sorrows of the human race
  Climb to the glory of the holiest place,
In this dread hour of travail, from earth's womb.
The pearly gates are dim; the voice of doom
  Sounds in God's halls; the seraph guard his
    face
  Veils with bent wing—the Father's Throne of
    Grace
Lies darkened by the shadow of the Tomb.
  Oh father, mother, hast thou known the pain
When Death has torn thy child from thine embrace,
Out of thine heart, and left the bleeding place
  Aching with emptiness, ne'er filled again?
    Oh father, mother, know the Love of God,
    Who, striking, bent Himself before the rod.

EASTER.

" FEAR NOT !" Oh, gracious words in love addressed
 To loving souls, who, ere the morn was gray,
 Had wandered to the sepulchre where lay
The body of their Lord.   To hearts oppressed
With nameless grief—their shadowy faith at best
 But an unfathomed sentiment, a ray
 Of struggling sunlight which had gone astray
'Midst the dark clouds that filled each anxious
   breast—-
 Ye came, the Herald of the Easter dawn :
And straight the clouds of doubt asunder fled
 Even as youthful morning, scattering night,
 Laughs back from waving wood and dewy lawn -
Warming with love the hearts now chill with
   dread.
  Sweet words, " Fear not " dawn of Eternal
   Light !

ASCENSION.

He lifted up His hands and blessed them, then
   Rose from the wondering earth in wingless
      flight,
Leaving His blessing with the sons of men,
   Swept with their sorrows to the starry height,
Passed with the scars their sins had made, again,
   Into His home of everlasting light :
Rose with their sins, until, beyond their ken,
   A distant cloud received Him from their
      sight.
Lo ! I am with you alway : this the word,
   The last the Saviour spake, when still His
      hand
Trembled in blessing o'er the sorrowing band.
Oh Jesu, with us alway, blessed Lord,
   With us on earth in Purity and Love,
   With us, and we in God with Thee above !

WHITSUNDAY.

WHITE daisies lighten all the sward, and bright
   Heaven smiles with fleecy cloudlets.   Every
      breeze
   Shakes as it laughs through the blossom-laden
      trees
Petals of snow upon the grass.   To-night
The white moon, looking from the zenith's height,
   Will trace a white road o'er the pathless seas.
   (Think on the mystery of mysteries !)
Even the bloody thorn doth blossom white !
   White by the washing of the Holy Ghost.
My soul and body I present to Thee,
A living sacrifice.   Oh Lord, lift me
   Into the number of Thy heavenly host,—
White souls, whose everlasting antiphon
Swells its deep music round the Great White
      Throne !

TRINITY SUNDAY.

Oh hoary earth, whose whirling sphere doth roll
  In self-contain'd energy for ever,
Praise the great Triune God till thy steadfast pole
  With the deep music of His praise shall quiver.
Shout, storm-rent peaks, deep glens, plains—let the
      whole
  Vast continent praise Him ; ocean, lake, and river
Thunder your anthems : clouds on high unroll
  Your streamers ; winds, praise ye the great Breath-
      giver.
One sphere, one earth, in wondrous orbit sweeping
  On through the void immense, for ever on,
  Land, ocean, and the trembling air's blue zone.
One God Father, Creator, in whose keeping
  All dwell ; one Christ, whose waters wash from
      wrong,
  Life-giving Spirit, fill our souls with song !

SPRINGTIDE AND SUMMER.

I was a work-worn student,
  Aweary of books and men,
And I came for rest and refreshment
  Where the burn sings down the glen.
She was a winsome bairnie,
  Fresh as her wind-swept skies,
And the light of five merry springtides
  Danced in her sunny eyes.

*　　*　　*　　*

Mine was a cold, hard manhood
  A woman my heart had slain,
Twelve years was it dead and buried
  Ere I came to the glen again.
She was a soft-eyed lassie,
  Sweet as her native brae,
And the love of her seventeen summers
  Bloomed like the earth in May.

*　　*　　*　　*

F

I am an old gray traveller,
  But my heart is fresh and free,
And young as the hearts of the children
  That sport at the old man's knee.
She, many a springtide and summer,
  Hath brought me sunshine and flower,
And sweeter the years have made her,
  But older—never an hour !

THE LAST TOKEN.

He bent from his saddle and kissed me again, and
    whispered a soft good-night,
Then touched his horse with the spur, and left me
    alone in the fading light ;
He turned in his saddle upon the hill and waved me
    a last good-bye,
Where horse and man loomed black against the glow
    of the sunset sky.

I stood alone by the garden gate, and heard. through
    the evening still,
Borne hither the sound of his horse's hoofs as he
    plunged down the stony hill ;
I heard him splash through the little brook where it
    straggles across the lane,
And sharply the hoofs rang out on the road as he
    climbed to the moor again :

Fainter and fainter, melting at last in the depths of
the summer night,—

Melting as melt in the gathering eve all shapes from
the straining sight ;

And the Earth breathed forth her sweetness to the
evening breeze's sigh,

But naught was sweet as his kiss or soft as the
whisper of his good-bye.

I knew not why, but my heart was afraid. yet morn
would bring him again,

So I tried to smile at the shapeless fears and laugh
at my self-born pain :

But I could not laugh, for my heart was full, my
eyes were waiting to weep,

As I sat me down by the cradle-side to sing our
babe to sleep.

'Twas midnight past and the moon had set ere to
my bed I crept,

But all my sense was awake in dreams through all
the hours I slept ;

Oh, the horror of that galloping, that galloping over
the heath,

With my husband dragged at the stirrup, and sobbing
out his breath.

I was tied to the saddle, and he, he was dragged o'er
the moor on his back,

And the horse was a devil and laughed aloud as he
heard my heart-strings crack—

He cried for death, and he could not die; then
under the horse's feet,

In his cradle all flushed with sleep, I saw my baby
sweet.

I saw—next moment the black hoof fell—down,
down on his rose-leaf face,

And left oh, Christ!——My soul sprang up and
shook the fell dream from its place,

And the sun was laughing in thro' the leaves, and
baby was laughing too,

Her mother's morning greeting from her eyes of
forget-me-not blue.

And I smiled and shook my fears off, the chill horror
of the night,
And clasped my baby to my breast, and laughed with
the morning's light.
I waited all that day and sang, and waited on till late,
And waited on till midnight beside the garden gate:

And waited, till the stars turned pale before the rising
sun,
Waited, until he rode on high and the new day was
begun,
Waited, until the clouds drove up and broke in
thunder and rain,
Waited—ah, waited for his kiss—but he never came
again.

*   *   *   *   *

Five years are past and gone since then, they say, and
it may be so,
I know not if they be years or weeks, nor how they
come or go:

And they bring me a message, a last good-bye. from
    the hand of the long-mourned dead
They bring me a handkerchief, yellow with age. and
    dabbled with faded red.

MISERERE.

A BOAT went sailing, sailing down
   The track of the setting sun.
And the waves broke red, as she dipped her head
   Into them one by one :—
     Dying, a-dying,
  Alack ! the sweet day lay a-dying.

A lass stood gazing, gazing forth,
   Hard by the old pier-stair,
And the sunset glow from the wave below
   Lived in her wealth of hair :—
     Praying, a-praying,
  Well-a-day ! the sweet maid stood a-praying.

The boat went sailing, sailing down,
   And hull, and sail, and spar,
Ere the day was run, 'gainst the broad red sun
   Loomed black and clear afar :—
     Dying, a-dying,
  Alack ! the sweet day lay a-dying.

And the lass stood watching, watching there,
   Till the lingering day did die,
And the moon did grow, while the sunset glow
   Was fading out of the sky :—
     Fading, a-fading,
Well-a-day ! the sweet light was a-fading.

A spirit rose sighing, sighing aloft,
   She breathed the waters o'er
With a sob, the wild Death of the Tempest's breath,
   And the mist-shroud over the shore :—
     Wailing, a-wailing,
The dead men's souls were a-wailing.

The boat was battling, battling with
   The pitiless ocean there,
And the maid strained her sight, through the gloom
   of night.
   And rent her soul with prayer :—
     Breaking, a-breaking,
Two lovers hearts were a-breaking.

And one was fighting, fighting the waves,
   Out in the tempest's gloom,
And one did pray her young life away
   Alone in her cheerless room :—
     Dying, a-dying,
Mary, Mother ! two souls are a-dying.

The sun was climbing, climbing up,
   From the merry East looked he,
And a lass lay dead on her snow-white bed,
   And a lad slept on the sea :—
     Singing, a-singing,
Two souls in Heaven were singing !

AVE MARIA.

The sun rode high in the merrye blue sky,
  The birdés did sing in the greenwood free,
Mayd Marye knelt at the Holye well
Beside the Cross, and her beads did tell,
  And warbled a " Hail, Marye ! "

Oh, the month was May, when, as I've heard say,
  The birdés pair in the greenwood free,
And I wis tall Will was a yeoman bold,
And it was not a prayer that the yeoman told
  When he whispered his " Hail, Marye ! "

Oh, the Holye well did chime like a bell,
  The birdés sang all in the greenwood free,
But none nesang sweet as the youth and the
    mayd,
When under the Cross their troth they sayd,
  And chaunted their " Hail, Marye ! "

SEA TREASURES.

I HEARD the children's voices through all the
summer day,
And the languorous air was merry with the music
of their play,
While the measured thud of distant oars came o'er
the ocean wide,
Merrily rang the childish laugh to the lap of the
flowing tide.

The sun was climbing down the West, the shadows
grew and grew,
And the listless ocean murmured, as the tired earth
breathed anew ;
Sweetly the little voices chimed, as I lay in the
window there,
'Midst roses, jasmine, and tendrilled plants, that
swayed in the evening air.

Murmured the moving ocean on, rustled the leaves
in the breeze,
Rising and falling the measured thud of oars came
over the seas,
Nodded the heavy-petalled rose, as the wind
breathed fresh and free,
But the children's voices were hushed—were hushed
—not a note floated in to me.

Were hushed, save once that a plaintive wail rose
from the murmuring shore,
And died, like the swash of the broken wave when
it seeks the deep once more ;
But the wail was echoed in my breast, till it choked
the rising prayer,
Till the ocean gasped with unborn shrieks, that
mocked the silent air.

Still silent !—I could not move to see—yet I was a
mother, too,
Knew well how little voices prattle all the daytime
through :

Too weak to stir, too weak to cry and the minutes
    passed in years,
I listened—listened till my heart was throbbing in
    mine ears.

And then the gravel garden path crunched 'neath
    a shuffling tread,
A moment, and the door flew wide they brought
    me in my dead :
And a crowd of solemn little faces circled all around,
My little face was smiling as they laid it on the
    ground.

Dead ! with the laugh upon her lips, that late sang
    through the air,
Shells in the tiny hand, a crown of seaweed on her
    hair ;
Dead ! the sweet eyes that lit my life to shine above
    the sky,
Aye, dead—oh. God ! and Death itself not half so
    dead as I !

A SPRING DAY.

Bright sun and wind-swept sky,
Melting shadows passing by,
Shadows of fleecy clouds floating on high.

Clear air and joyous breeze,
Frolic breath, that through the trees
Laughs to the groans of their sad symphonies.

Splash, splash—the wind-born wave
Sings the song its mother gave,
Sinking in foam to its sand-mantled grave.

Sweet, sweet—the lark remote
Carols clear, with tireless throat,
Sings to the sunshine that taught him his note.

Glad heart that lov'st the spring,
Thou, like Nature, learn'st to sing,
Praising thy Maker for everything.

REST.

On, the rill, the new-born rill,
  Laughter and music, it danceth by.
Leaping its way down the thyme-scented hill ·
      Aye,
    Merrily rings the child's laugh on high.
    But what is a laugh to such as I?

Oh, the stream, the maiden stream,
  In eddying smiles its shallows lie,
Living in shadowy deeps its dream :
      Aye,
    Sweet alike, maiden's smile and sigh.
    But what are they twain to such as I?

Oh, the river, the mighty river,
  Breasting the sunlight its currents fly,
Bulrushes tall on its margin quiver ;
      Aye,
    Strong flows the stream of Manhood by.
    But what is Manhood to such as I?

Oh, the sea, the boundless sea,
  Rolling for ever beneath the sky,
Changeless its deeps as Eternity;
        Aye,
  Quiet there is for those who die,
And God hath sleep for such as I.

A MAY CAROL.

Oh, the merry Maytime,
  The merry May!
The flowers looked up to the smiling sun,
And they laughed because the spring was begun,
  All in the month of May.
But the north wind blew, all gray was the sky.
  Alack and well-a-day!
And the flowers were frozen, and some did die,—
Die, die, did droop and die.
  Oh, the merry May!

Oh, the merry Maytime,
  The merry May!
The trees did smile in their fresh young green,
And sang, when the breezes danced in between,
  All in the month of May.

But the trees were sad, and the leaves turned black.
Alack and well-a-day !
And they groaned when the north wind swept on
his track,—
Laughing fierce, roared down his track.
Oh, the merry May !

Oh, the merry Maytime.
The merry May !
The woods with the little birds' voices rang.
They twittered to Earth. but to Heaven they sang.
All in the month of May.
But the fierce wind scattered the snow on the earth.
Alack and well-a-day !
And the starving songsters forgot their mirth,—
Mirth. mirth, forgot their mirth.
Oh, the Merry May !

Oh, the merry Maytime.
The merry May !
Ah ! lovers' hearts were so full that they
Said all with their eyes, and had naught else to say.
All in the month of May.

But the hearts grew cold in the winter blast,
     Alack and well-a-day!
And eyes were speechless, but words came fast,—
Many and fast, for love, too fast.
     Oh, the merry May!

     Oh, the merry Maytime,
      The merry May!
The children sing as the breeze blows along,
And the old man laughs to hear their song,
     All in the month of May.
But cold the icy shadow doth pass,
     Alack and well-a-day!
And babe and gray-beard sleep 'neath the grass —
Gray head and golden beneath the grass.
     Oh, the merry May!

TO E——.

Oh, the sun was bright and the sky was blue,
   And the wind blew fresh adown lane and lea,
And silver the clouds that before it flew,
   While the light came dancing over the sea.

Oh, the year was young, and the life of Spring
   Was stirring the buds and the blossoms to birth,
For Winter had folded his rime-covered wing,
   And the springtide was climbing the merry round
     earth.

Oh, the birds they twittered so blithely, for they
   Gathered the sunshine to shed it in song :
Oh, the hours were but minutes that danced to their
     lay,
   But precious as years as they hurried along.

Oh, sun and blue sky, wind on wave, lane and lea,
   Oh, the flush on thy cheek and the light in thine eye,
Oh, the song of the birds and the dance of the sea,—
   But thou wast the sunshine, the song, and the sky.

SUNSHINE.

A narrow bar of sunshine
   Stretched across the floor,
For the summer morn was smiling
   Through the half-closed cottage door.
The sheep-dog lay athwart it,
   And blinked his drowsy eyes:
In the pathway of the sunbeam
   Buzzed the busy flies.

A wooden cradle stopped it,
   It would not be denied,
But kissed the baby fingers
   Above the cradle-side.
It climbed to the old brown rafters
   Over the baby's bed,
And he crowed, and stretched his hands out
   For the sunbeam overhead.

Singing a baby ballad,
  Down on the shady floor,
To the click of her flying needles.
  To the sea-voice from the shore :
Bare-legged, and brown, and healthy,
  Brown hair brightening with gold,
There sat the baby's mother,
  Scarce twenty summers old.

All on the floor in the shadow,
  Girlish and fresh and clean,
Singing her verses, with sometimes
  A little sigh between :
For life was a little dreary,
  The wave was sad on the shore,
And only a little sunbeam
  Stole through the half-closed door.

So she sighed. The babe crows louder,
  The dog springs up, a shade
Blots out the little sunbeam.
  Blots out the path it made ;

Then down go knitting and needles
(Alas for the work undone !),
She stands in a flood of sunlight—
Her sailor has brought the sun.

METAMORPHOSIS.

In the garden's furthest corner,
  A wild rose-tree grew;
Unmarked, it bloomed in summer,
  And slept the winter through.

One day the gardener saw it,
  And cut and trimmed it round,
Then took it from its corner
  To plant in kindlier ground.

With cruel knife he pierced it
  Down to its heart, and then
A bud in the wound he planted,
  And bound it up again.

And the little bud—oh, wonder !—
  Drinks up the sap and grows,
And gives, for the wild white blossom,
  The wealth of a perfect rose.

My rose-bud—so the great Gardener
Planted thy life in mine,
And all the buds of my manhood
And all its flowers are thine.

THE SONG OF THE SEA.

THE song of the sea, the song of the sea,
Tell me, what is its burden to thee,
Dancing in glee
'Neath the cloud-splashed heaven breezy and free—
The song of the sea?

The song of the sea, the song of the sea,
It sings of my childhood, far, far away,
When life was a spring-song, a flower-gathering lay,
When the year was all May,
And the day was all play,
And night but the shadow of lovelier day ;
It laugheth to me,
As the white-crested wavelets come over the bay—
The song of the sea.

The song of the sea, the song of the sea,
Tell me, what is its burden to thee,
So solemnly,
In the moonbeams sighing its soft melody—
The song of the sea?

The song of the sea, the song of the sea—
Oh, carols and sighs through a scent-laden air,
Oh, a breast that trembled, yet laughed at care ;
       To ask why so fair,
       My heart did not dare,
Till another heart answered my unspoken prayer ;
       It sigheth to me,
When the moon shines out on the ocean there—
       The song of the sea.

The song of the sea, the song of the sea,
       Tell me what is its burden to thee,
              When furiously
The storm-demon rides 'neath his cloud canopy—
       The song of the sea?

The song of the sea, the song of the sea,
When the wild howling winds drive the billows
       before,
And the deep thunder peals through their unceasing
       roar,
       And the fierce lightnings pour
       From Heaven's open door,

Swift gleaming on rock, wave, and surf-beaten shore;
  It shrieketh to me—
Oh, God! how it calls back that horror once more—
  The song of the sea.

 The song of the sea, the song of the sea,
 Tell me, what is its burden to thee,
   As sullenly
The long swell booms on the sandy lee—
  The song of the sea?

 The song of the sea, the song of the sea,
It tells of a morrow, but not of a morn,
It tells of the daylight, but not of the dawn,
  Of a youth of youth shorn,
  Of a love of love lorn,
Of a memory-tombed soul from its living corpse torn
  It waileth to me
Of a life that was only a thing to be worn—
  The song of the sea.

A YARN.

Mates, I wor standin' 'longside my gun, a ready to
  let un go
  With his cargo of grape for the Frenchman. I wor
  ready to fire, I say,
When the smoke cleared off from my port a bit, and,
  Lord love yer, I see the foe
  Not thirty fathoms to starboard, with his foretop
  shot away.

I can see 'un now—his soldier-devils a rattlin' away
  from the tops,
  And the skipper a walkin' the quarter-deck all
  ablaze with crosses and stars,
His guns, and the faces that peered through the
  ports—when up the riggin' there pops
  A little yellow-curled chap, as bold as the boldest
  of British tars.

He waved his cap, and shouted out summut that I
    couldn't understand,
    But the Froggies laughed, and I heard him laugh as
      clear as a bell at sea ;
An' I couldn't a fired that gun, mates, I dursn't a
    moved my hand,
    For I thought of my own little youngster at home
      that rode on his daddy's knee.

An' I wouldn't a made that gun speak up if you'd
    give me a thousand pound :
    But I hadn't no need, and I thanks the Lord as sent
      me a message of lead
What struck me amidships, and down on the deck by
    my gun I drops in a swound,
    And Davy Jones pretty nigh had me, for my mess-
      mates thought I wor dead.

When I wakes up, for I didn't know nothink for days
    or weeks mayhap,
    I hears how we crammed them Frogs' stomachs with
      grub for a bit, d'ye see ?

But this is the best of that fight, I thinks, as I sits
   with my boy in my lap,
That if that little French chap wor killed, he never
   wor killed by me.

MY BABY'S FINGER.

A BABY'S finger, one pink rose-leaf rolled
   Into a finger, tipped with a tiny shell,
   Here pointing, there, and everywhere. What spell
Draws forth that wondering index? To behold
Thy little world of marvels, all untold,
   With thy great eyes, and all the thoughts to tell
   That point thy finger, content were I to dwell
In the blue depths that thy pure soul enfold.
So point pink rose-leaf; whither wilt thou lead
   My curious eye?——Ah, no, I cannot gaze
   Where thy pure vision soars, the dazzling rays
Burn my foul eyes, and pain is all their meed.
   Oh baby dear, were I clean as thou art,
   I too might see myself in Jesus' heart.

TO THE SEA.

SEA, that now laugh'st along thy pebbly strand
 In infant billows, sporting with the shore,
 Kissing it into splendour, as they pour
Their broken floods up to the sunlit land ;
Or, as by breath of summer morning fanned,
 Thou quiverest, golden, at day's eastern door,
 Or slumbering, waveless, o'er thy ribbèd floor,
Or heaving, touched by a dead wind's ghostly hand—
Art *thou* untrue, thou beautiful, art thou
 The same whose windless deeps yawn black behind
 Each tempest-driven surge, what time the wind
Shrieketh Death's battle-cry ? Canst laugh as now
 Compassing death ? Art thou a truth, oh Sea,
 Or but a dream that only seems to be ?

THE SEA'S ANSWER.

Man, I am not a dream, I work and rest
  As I am bidden, work and rest for thee.
  The rivers thou defilest come to me,
Losing their foulness on my billowy breast,
And when my storm-wave lifts its angry crest,
  It warreth with the world's impurity.
  Even when my waters sleep along the lee,
My tides move, cleansing, at the moon's behest.
I am no dream, thou man, all true am I,
  Alike to breeze and tempest—when the light
  Glads my broad bosom, or the star-spread night
Glows in my wave, as in its sapphire sky.
  True to all nature, man, I am—be thine
  True to thy task to be as I to mine.

A DREAM OF GREAT STATESMEN.

MARCH, 1885.

I LAY, when summer shadows eastward crept,
 Upon the strand, and, as they longer grew,
Watched the rose-tinted cloudlets, where they slept
 Against the changing blue.

For I was weary of the wordy strife,
 The party fallacies' unvarying ring,
Poured through the teeming press, and my tired life
 Sought Nature's quieting.

And, for a while, the knowledge of the lie
 That underlay those patriots' words of fire,
Making the people's weal a party cry
 To hoist themselves the higher,

Charged all my heart with scorn.   In every land
  I saw the true, the noble, and the brave
Pass banished, slandered, struck by treacherous hand,
    Dishonoured, to the grave.

I saw the foul, exalted on the throne,   .
  Shine like a god upon the clamouring fools
Who scorned the pure, yet felt no shame to own
    Themselves the tyrant's tools.

And blood was spilled upon the senate floor,
  And scaffold saw-dust drank the life of kings,
And corpses blocked the council chamber door
    With voiceless murmurings.

Red war amid the harvest-sheaves was hurled,
  And myriads armed them at the despot's nod,
The blood-steam from the shambles of the world
    Rose in the sight of God.

E'en sanctuary was violate—from blood
   Not Zeus himself might cleanse his frighted fane,
And dark, beneath the shadow of the rood,
     Christ's altar saw the stain.

And creeping serpent-like from age to age,
   Moved hireling dagger, poison-cup, and gold,
And woman's traitor eyes, from every page,
     Smiled death upon the bold.

Ever the same dark tale of crime would tell
   The guileful Greek, the Viking on the wave :
Fierce Attila and wily Machiavel
     Alike sought to enslave.

Thus pondering, at the westward gate of day
   The sky blushed faintly to the kiss of night ;
Above, infrequent in the deepening gray,
     The coy stars glimmered white.

Now, o'er the sea night's sapphire æther crept.
  The dead day's rosy glimmer trembled still
On every wave.	Then mellow moonbeams leaped
    Over the eastward hill ;

A breeze once stirred the slumber of the sea,
  Wafted a scent of flowers and new-mown hay—-
A white sail crossed the moonlight—suddenly
    The soft scene passed away.

I stood amid a whirling sea of cloud,
  Dank, dark, by a moist south-wester landward driven,
And fitful wind-rents in the scudding shroud
    Opened the lurid heaven.

And distant thunder growled in cloudy caves,
  Wind shook the robe of mist from the troubled main,
Where columned clouds hurled on the seething waves
    Forked fire and furious rain.

The squall passed, fell the wind, save when it swept
   Over the shivering sea, and moaning died
Among the ruined cliffs, and closer crept
      The black mists' chilling tide.

And shadowy forms were there, that came and passed,
   Gigantic, melting in the rolling shroud,—
Forms that I knew, yet knew not, thick and fast,
      Peopling the silent cloud.

And, as I gazed, the walls of mist rolled back,
   Three mighty rainbows spanned the wrathful sky,
Beneath them hung the sun, in the cloudy rack,
      A blood-red globe on high.

A plain stretched limitless around, o'ergrown
   With funeral cypresses ; their boughs beneath
Lay storied vestiges of glory flown,
      Gray witnesses for Death.

And tottering-tower, and roofless fane, each told
    Its silent history of long ago ;
And dead kings' homes, where dead kings' hearths
      lay cold,
        Stood in the lurid glow.

And all the air was heavy with a moan,
    The leafy gloom stood shivering as it fell,
Each crumbling ruin held a stifled groan,
      Each stone a frozen knell.

And all the voices of the many things
    Rolled into one great echo of the Past,
Stirred the dull air, like myriad mighty wings,
      Into a mighty blast.

A mighty blast of one great voice, that bound
    My soul in spell to the strange words it said,
Swept in the vortex of the solemn sound,
      " Come up and see the dead."

Threading the dank, dark ruins, here and there,
  Wandered strange forms, nor rested ever.   Now
Trod loftily a man of kingly air,
      Of more than kingly brow.

Unchanging lustre from his fearless eyes
  Shone, as the moonbeam in a waveless lake
In liquid splendour looks from the mirrored skies.
      While slowly thus he spake :—

" 'Twas I who by the people's fickle train
  Was driven from my native city, thrust
Forth by the race I served with blood and brain,
      Because men called me just.

" While he who earned their plaudits "——" Yea,
    indeed,"
  Quoth one who stepped from out the ruins' shade ;
" He won because his wit taught him to read
      The men the gods had made."

I turned and saw him stand—one arm was flung
    Careless about a ruined column's base ;
One arm the mellow current of his tongue
      Followed with easy grace.

Scornful his eyes, as gushed his measured speech,
    Like fountain from his smiling lips,—" Who can
With the cold wand of distant Justice reach
      The seething heart of man ?

" Oh pedant Justice, cast thy scales away,
    Or, stay, weigh each his neighbour's goods, and then,
Though all thy weights be false, none will gainsay
      The boon thou art to men !

" I knew no virtue but the human breast,
    Upon the people's heart I laid my hand,
And learned its pulses.   I might bid it rest,
      Might bid it shake the land.

" *Men* felt I was a *Man*.   I learned to trace
   By my desires and passions, theirs ; but thou
Wouldst sit a god to rule the human race,
     With Justice on thy brow."

He spake, and passed.   Then, through the solemn
     place,
   Up to my side an armèd warrior came,
Tall as a god, with sad yet steadfast face,
     Lit by the sacred flame.

One whose clear eye could see the patriot's goal,
   One whose strong hand might shape the course of
     Fate,
One whose stern will first taught him self-control,
     Then served to guide the State.

His voice now murmured as a woodland stream,
   Now thundered with the storm-tossed ocean's roar :
A whisper from a love-lorn maiden's dream,
     The shout of gods at war.

" Mine was the hand that crowned my Fatherland
    With deathless beauty—bade, from age to age,
Her mighty name in glowing letters stand
      Upon the historic page.

" Yet men, my friend, to great Athené dear,
    Taught by herself to mould her form aright,
Murdered, beneath the shadow of her spear,
      Because he sought the Light.

" With foul disgrace they spattered my fair fame :
    Little I recked.   But when the accusing knife,
'Held by a bigot fool, struck at her name,—
      My Day, my Breath, my Life,—

" To fools and thieves I pleaded for my love,
    With tears and burning words of agony
Wrung from my lacerated heart.   I strove
      Even on bended knee,

" And thieves and fools were won.   The gods had laid
   Fire on my lips to burn their lies.   Once more
I lived, my name the fickle people made
      Resound from shore to shore."

He ceased, and as his voice's melody
   Died, and sad Echo sang its requiem,
My heart-strings trembled to her tender sigh,
      Breathed softly over them.

'Twas not his words, over their channel poured
   A music-river, till my amazèd sense
Could naught but hear   my soul an answering chord
      Swept by his eloquence.

While yet the echoes lingered, sudden broke
   A burst of martial music on mine ear,
The measured tramp of warrior thousands woke
      My startled sense to hear.

And in the lurid beam glowed lance and crest,
   Brands flashed blood-dipped round standards
      reared on high,
The deep notes of a mighty psalm confessed
      Jehovah's majesty.

" Unnameable, about whose veilèd throne
   Chained lightnings wait and silent thunders dwell,
Praise in the Height be given to Thee alone,
      Thou God of Israel !

" Let the sword praise Thee, drunk with Gentile gore,
   Let its ensanguined point Thy name of wrath
Write on their temples, till they strive no more,
      Lord God of Sabaoth !

" The stars Thy diadem, Almighty One,
   Thy shield the Sun, Thy sword the fires of Hell,
Praise in the Height be given to Thee alone,
      Thou shield of Israel !

" Let the fierce vulture, as his talons tear

   Kings' entrails, quivering flesh from snowy limbs

Of tender virgins, for his royal fare,

      Praise Thee in sounding hymns !

" Thy robe the rainbow, and Thy voice's tone

   Like the great water-floods that rage and swell,

Praise in the Height be given to Thee alone,

      Thou Word of Israel !

" Smite them,—old, young, wife, maiden, tender child :

   Spare not the smiter, glut the hungry sword,

Let the defiler's daughters be defiled,

      Avenge Thy people, Lord !

" O awful Light, whose faint reflex so shone

   On Moses' brow, that none might brook the spell,

Praise in the Height be given to Thee alone,

      Thou Light of Israel !

" Watch, gentle moon, that look'st o'er Zion's hill,
   Our slumbering wives and little ones to-night,
Smile them sweet dreams, thou lamp of God, until
     The day leaps into light.

" Oh Thou whose name is Strength, to Thee alone
   We leave our homes and those we love so well,
Stretch forth Thy hand to shield them.   Thee we own,
     Thee our Emmanuel."

The echoing thunders of the deep refrain
   Down columned depths of ruined temples rolled,
'Till the pale shadows in each startled fane
     Shrank back into the mould.

And one I marked beneath whose crownèd crest
   And shaggy brows the soul broke into light,
A snowy beard swept down where, on his breast,
     The mystic gems burned bright.

I

His voice was like the oracles of God
　　Thundering from Sinai's lightning-shivered height :
He spake, the people worshipped--where he trod
　　The craven learned to fight.

"God was my Strength, my Rock, my Shield, my
　　　Sword,
　　He taught His servant's feeble hands to war,
With the fierce lightnings of His changeless word
　　I smote His foes afar.

" He raised His hand, kings' hearts did melt with fear,
　　Their battled armies fled before His breath,
Walled cities shook at sight of Israel's spear—
　　He spake—His word was Death.

" By my frail hand He smote the Philistine,
　　Gaza and Ashdod heard Jehovah's name,
And broken gods and desecrated shrine
　　Fed the avenging flame.

"And David's city, whence the Syrian hold
　Frowned on the Temple, mine it was to win :
The smoke of sacrifice, burnt as of old,
　　Rose for a nation's sin.

" My people wrote my deeds on brass, to hang
　High on the mount of God, out-living Death :
My bosom warmed the snake, whose traitor fang
　　Should rob me of my breath.

" He sought my life, his was the treacherous sword
　Drank of the stream that warmed her heart whose
　　breast
Pillowed his faithless head—the festal board
　　Beheld the slaughtered guest.

" He slew his brethren with his traitor kiss
　Warm on their lips : butchered like sheep fell they,
My glorious sons, nor, dying, knew the bliss
　　Of the victorious fray.

" My best belovèd, child of mine age, thy eyes
  Looked into his through mine—my dying lips
Mingled thy name with Israel's destinies,
      Darkened by my eclipse.

" Oh child, whose infant prattle cooled my heart,
  Dry with stern statecraft, seared with the fire of war,
Whose maiden sweetness drew my soul apart,
      To rest in thy peaceful star :

" Oh land, whom this rough hand hath helped to bring
  Out of the darkness of thy slavery
By bloody travail, till thy mountains sing
      Their pæan of liberty :

" Oh daughter, can thy heart beat warm again
  Upon his breast who pierced thy father's side ?
Oh Zion, wilt thou crown the brow of Cain,
      And hail the parricide ? "

' Thine was my lot," quoth one who stood hard by,
  " I loved my people, sought to make them great ;
'Twas mine to live for them, 'twas mine to die
      Because I served the State.

" My order hated me, because I strove
  Not for them only, for the Roman race ;
The people loved me not, because my love
      Looked Justice in the face.

" I could not brook to see the noble's greed
  Crowd the plebeian from the public land ;
I claimed for all the right to live—my seed
      Died ere it left my hand,

" My law was strangled in its birth, my head
  Fell for its thoughts of right, my people, drunk
With jealousy, knew not my country bled
      When bled my headless trunk.

" The Volscian laughed to see his conqueror fall,
    The Equian now might leave his mountain home,
The trembling Latin manned his city wall,
        Nor dreamed of help from Rome.

" A parricide they called me.   Yet 'twas I,
    First of the Romans, sought the People's good,
Planted the tree of social liberty,
        Baptised it with my blood.

" Scattered my household gods, my body hurled
    From the Tarpeian rock, disgraced my name—
Down all the sounding centuries the world
        Shall peal with my deeds of fame."

He passed—passed too the Hebrew host, as fades
    The twilight's latest glimmer into night,—
Passed in the silence of the solemn shades,—
        Melted, unseen, from sight.

And cloistered court, vast hall, and columned aisle
  Rang to the tramp of armèd heel no more,
And the dank precincts of each hoary pile
    Lay voiceless as before.

Not even a shadow through the desolate place
  Floated—like an undying death it lay,
A widowed world that veiled its grief-stained face,
    Trembling before the day.

Sudden the leaden air was stirred to sound,
  A mighty voice swept through the murky sky,
Till the red twilight trembled, till the ground
    Quivered responsively.

" Where be the men that slew me ?—They are dead,
  Their names mere shadows of a bygone age;
But I—I live in the deathless lustre shed
    From my undying page.

" Dead, yet my words restore to me my breath,
   I am, I speak, till the world shall cease to be ;
Dead, their deeds damn them with a second death —
      A life of infamy.

" In vain thy bodkin, Fulvia, my piercèd tongue
   Shall plead, in the forum of the world, my cause,
Shall gain the verdict of the centuries, among
      The shouts of their applause.

" My severed head shall think when Rome is not,
   When thou and thine adulterous Antony
Are dust, the foulness of whose deeds doth rot
      The page of history."

" Peace, fool ! think'st thou thy words with deeds
   can vie ?
   E'en though thy words live on, the deeds lie dead,"
Spake one, the calm strength of whose steadfast eye
      Belied his hoary head.

" Deeds are the stones of statecraft patriots place
   Each in its rank to build the Republic's walls ;
Words but the pictures, hanging there to grace
     The sternness of its halls.

" Where be the deeds that built the state of Rome ?
   Not thine, vain man.   Go seek the mouldered dust
Of the true hearts that bled for hearth and home,
     Keeping a nation's trust.

" Venice, my love, my bride, my ocean gem,
   My Aphrodite of the Adrian wave,
Long bear thy brow the starry diadem
     Thy hero-children gave.

" My youth I yielded thee, my prime, my age,
   And thrice I mourned a son who died for thee ;
My last, thou traitress, gavest the traitor's wage—
     The name of infamy.

" My life of toil forgot, disgraced my name,
   They took my trust ; content, I bowed my head :
Upon the altar of my country's shame
      My heart lay bruised and dead.

" I loved her better than my love, but she
   Cast my love from her at a faction's nod :
One day my grieved soul sorrowed, the next soared free
      Up to my country's God."

His stately head was bowed, one hand was pressed
   On the smooth majesty of his lofty brow,
Closed were his eyes, his beard wrote on his breast
      His age in driven snow.

And, moved to see the venerable head
   Bowed o'er the memories of a saddened life ;
Mourning with him his children's bloody bed,
      Mourning the party strife,

That drave—an exile from his native land—
   His living son, and, to his country's shame,
Spurned the mild blessings of his father-hand,
      And spat upon his name,—

My heart flamed up, my veins, fed with its fire,
   Pulsed, till my swollen bosom strained in birth
Of high intent, and chivalrous desire
      To right the wrongs of earth.

My soul rose to my lips—then eyes and brain
   And sense reeled at the picture that they saw ;
My fierce words sank to nothingness again,
      I stood in silent awe.

For the red light flashed back from crested helm,
   From jewelled turban, mitre, coronet,—
The feather helmet of the Aztec's realm
      With Churchman's cap was met.

A thousand faces from a hundred lands,
  The mighty great and mean, who went before
Down the dread stream of Time, whose iron hands
    Of old the sceptre bore,

Thronged the ruin-cumbered plain.   Armed *cap-à-pie*
  I saw the feudal warrior-chief, the man
Who on men's bodies forged his policy
    In the roaring battle's van.

Here was the prelate, whose unworldly thought
  Gorged his gross Church with the fat lands he stole
From the fool-king, who deemed them richly bought
    With masses for his soul:

Here was the prince who bent his saintly knees
  So oft in prayer he ne'er could rise to rule,
Content, so he could take his prayerful ease,
    To be a faction's tool:

The chemist-statesman of the Papal Court
  Who steered the ship of State with the phial of
    death,
Greeted the honoured guest with smiling port,
    And smiled away his breath :

The man who thought it death the weak to wrong,
  But boldly dared the mighty to the strife ;
And he who crushed the small, but for the strong
    Hired the assassin's knife :

The king who held the sceptre of his Lord,
  And meted justice to an adoring folk,
Whose hymn of freedom, when he drew his sword,
    Slavery's fetters broke :

Christ's Vicar, servant of servants, he whose hold
  Upon the keys of Heaven is his boast ;
Yet thought no wrong to change God's grace for gold,
    To sell the Holy Ghost.

There was the mighty Cardinal who shed
   The noblest blood in France to build her throne,
Before whose glance conspiracy fell dead,
      Whose stern will ruled alone ;

Who raised his country's name, and broke the sway
   Of the haughty house of Hapsburg, humbled Spain,
His country's nobles taught how to obey,
      Her monarchs how to reign.

Cromwell was there, his visage scarred and lined
   With the stern mastery of his passionate soul,
Th' embodiment of Will itself, mankind
      Ruling by self-control.

Such was his brow what time, at Marston fight,
   Fierce Rupert's chivalry before him broke ;
Such when brave Leslie's legions, hurled in flight,
      Vanished like wind-driven smoke.

Not these alone—but many a mighty name
  Glowed on my 'wildered sense, as sight did trace
The features of the glorious dead, who came
    Into that deathly place.

And many a picture from the buried past
  Leaped into life out of the tomb of Time ;
No formless shade, from History's pages cast
    Hoar with the ages' rime,

But passing in my sight, clear to my eyes
  As the deeds of our dull Now ; as one may see
The Alpine summits pierce the azure skies
    Of sunny Italy,

A hundred ages old, yet evermore
  Fresh as they left the workshop of their God—
So the Dead lived before me as of yore,
    Spurning the burial sod.

They thronged the avenues of sense, mine ears
  Borrowed of my full eyes, their voices shed
Into my soul the very hopes and fears
    That swayed the mighty Dead.

Great Chatham, passing, touched me : by my side
  Talleyrand lingered : I started where I stood,
As through the press I saw, like serpent, glide
    Robespierre, man of blood—

The gory handkerchief beneath his chin.
  Then reeled my brain. Blood, blood, there seemed
    to be
Naught save a blood-red storm-cloud, closing in
    A stretch of bloody sea.

Great names fell on my amazèd ear.   I heard
  Metternich, Cavour, through a storm of sound—
The roar of cannon, the clash of arms that stirred
    Even the steadfast ground :

The shout of victory, the widow's moan,
  The grand *Te Deum*, and the dirge of woe,
The mob's fierce roar that shook the storied throne,
    All, all did pass and flow

Into the lap of sleep.—A breath of air
  Touched my hot cheek, unsealed my eyelids; I
Saw the sea quivering in the moonbeams there,
    Under the starry sky.

The rise and fall of Ocean's bosom bore
  The silver pathway to the land, and shed
Soft moonlight, glittering all along the shore,
    Round every wavelet's bed.

Th' unequal rhythm of their music lapped
  My senses in its sweetness. Starry eyes
Called me from Heaven, till my spirit, rapt,
    Rose to the sapphire skies.

K

So still, so pure, so sweet,—half dreamily,
　　I lay and wondered: had I passed Death's stream?
Was this God's rest from battle, lulling me
　　　　Into a blissful dream?

For the red vision of that bloody sea
　　And all the horrors that racked my breast with pain
Were all too true, too fearful true to be
　　　　A nothing of the brain.

And slowly all the music of the night
　　Quickened my spirit.　But awakened thought,
Yet darkened by the dream, for inner light
　　　　Amid its shadows sought.

And seeking thus, my mind was drawn aside
　　To view the statecraft of the present day—
My country's policy, the men who guide
　　　　England upon her way.

Why were they great, the men whose sceptres' light
    Flashes down all the years of history ?
One single aim the secret of their might,
        A single policy.

They saw their goal, where none around might see ;
    They held the track, when others wandered, failed ;
Their friends were strengthened by their constancy ;
        Their foes before them quailed.

What is our rulers' aim ? One aim ! nay, say
    A thousand, rather : such a maze, no man
May find the clue, but, searching, wastes the day,
        And ends where he began.

None fear to speak, to write,—the Deluge were
    A very puddle to the wordy flood
That waters the wine of manhood, and bids fair
        To water English blood.

Ay, speak—or truth or lies, and should they fall
   Upon resentful ears, our Patriot must
Cry them a mercy, his hot words recall,
     And grovel in the dust.

But act—they never *act*, they can but drive.
   Like a rudderless ship : yet wondrous how they
    boast,
If the wind change and save the crew alive
     From the death-threatening coast !

God, one would think they made the wind !—and
    speech
   And journal vaunt the name of one great man,
Whose arm might sweep the stars within his reach,
     The chasm of death might span.

And while they prate, in Europe, where of old
   One word from England framed a policy,
Men sneer at her wind-bag statesmen, and make bold
     To pass their protests by.

Afraid to draw the sword to right the wrong,
  Afraid to raise the shield the weak to save,
They plod, the weary waste of words among,
      The path to Honour's grave.

And loathsome Slavery creeps back to day,
  And Superstition marshals all her bands,
And Greed of Conquest takes her savage way,
      With blood-bedabbled hands.

The murdered mother, at whose milkless breast
  Her wailing infant seeks its life in vain,
The flames devouring the deserted nest,
      When all the birds are slain :

Thy sons who fell because they met too few
  The enemies thy rulers made, the ally
Who kept his troth, deeming thy promise true,
      And lost his liberty,—

Cry to thee, England,   and thy leaders stand
    Lamenting men's dishonesty and greed,
And tearfully proclaim throughout the land
        Their mild and peaceful creed.

" Oh, that all men would learn of us," they cry,
    " Bend to the storm and let it pass ; we learn,
In the calm heights of our morality,
        Even success to spurn.

" Failure to scorn, to know no thing so great
    As some large principle, some sounding word,
A party shibboleth : for *that* the State
        Perchance might draw the sword."

While Wrong, that wont of old the light to shun,
    Stalks in the noonday with her devil's brood
Of grisly Horrors, till the saddened sun
        Looks down through the steam of blood.

Egypt a charnel—yet the word of Peace
    Was sent her—true, 'twas sped by a rifle-ball :
And Africa's down-trodden millions cease
    For England's aid to call.

Our Colonies insulted, scorned, until
    They doubt their mother, and our country rife
With social problems, threatening to spill
    The nation's very life.

Thus did my dream call on my waking sense
    To weigh the Present by the Past, till I
Grieved at the littleness that scrapes its pence
    And squanders history ;

Casts England's name and fame away, and fears
    To justify her claims by sword or pen,
Our hard-won heritage, all that endears
    England to Englishmen.

Not her long downs, where purple shadows chase
　The melting sunlight o'er their wind-swept flanks;
Her woods that stoop to kiss the river's face,
　　Laughing twixt flowery banks;

Not cliffs that echo to the ocean's roar,
　Nor mountain-cradled lakes, nor smiling meads
Make England—but the men who gird her shore
　　With everlasting deeds.

And, wearily, I cast the thought aside,
　Lifted my eyes.— O deeps immeasurable
Of light, stars that eternally abide,
　　Changeless, innumerable;

Oh light, so pure, the white moon's silver ray
　Is dross to thine,—so pure, that angel eyes
Might own thy lustre,—draw my soul away
　　Into thy Paradise!

The wave soft murmuring along the shore,
 The moonlight quivering on the open sea,
The white orb looking from her starry floor
    Whispered their peace to me;

Whispered their peace. The angel of the night
 Swift o'er the sapphire deeps of æther trod,
Filled my perplexèd soul with heavenly light,
    And bade it rest in God.

LYRICS OF A LOVE-TIME.

I.

Till merry May is here, my love,
  The day is fresh and bright ;
The gladness of the year, my love,
  Is passing into light.
The flowers blow around, my love,
  The birds sing merrily -
And colour, scent, and sound, my love,
  Are all for you and me !

II.

The November day with its sky of gray
  Wakes o'er the landscape, cold and drear ;
The glow of dawn that heralds the morn
  Is the hectic flush of the dying year.
Love, is the gray for you and for me?
    Do the wild winds sigh
    For me and for thee ?

To think that our youth must die, must die,
Like the waning year, solemnly, silently.
    Is the flush of our youth
But the hectic that shadows the sad old truth.
    That the seeds of Death
    Strike root, when we draw our earliest breath.
And that age is coming for you and for me?

III.

    Sun, cloud, and the restless sea,
    Cloud, sun, and the restless sea, —
Smiling sea in the purple shadow,
    Laughing sea in the broad sunlight,
Bright as the laughing green of the meadow,
    Sapphire blue as the deeps of night :
Clouds, with your shadows purple and gray,
Splash, splash the swift waves as they pour on their
        way.
Oh light and shadow ! Oh shadow and light !
Laugh ye and smile at the broken white

Of the waves as they dance to the wind's tuneful breath,

Gathering, breaking,

Sleeping, awaking,

Rising anew in the moment of death—
Sun, cloud, and the restless sea :
Light and shadow for you and for me.

IV.

Blazing sun and blazing sea,
Light ! light ! light !   is there light for me ?
Aye, a light that dazzles eye and brain,
A light that makes the darkness plain,
   The black night there in my heart.
Blazing sun and blazing sea,
Heat ! heat ! heat !   is there heat for me ?
Aye, a heat that burns like the fire of Hell,
Scorching my brain's remotest cell,
   Yet melting not the ice of my heart.
Oh, my heart is cold—cold—cold, love —
   My heart is dark--dark ;
I am growing old, love.

Hark !

There's a ripple of laughter in the silent street,
Two sunny-headed children, with bare, brown
        feet.
Blue-eyed, brown eyed, urchin and maid,
    Smiling smiles of coral and pearl,
Playing there in the narrow street's shade ;
      A young mother with them   only a girl
         All in the dust.
     Laughing all, in the dirt and dust
Of the dry gutter, laughing all three
Like a woodland stream : is this not sweet to
     thee.
    Is there *no* tear in that fevered eye ?
       No ! 'tis a lie,
    Mother and child will die.
See, the sexton, in the churchyard, pulls
Out of the mould three grinning skulls.
   Where is now the laughing eye ?
     List, for the rippling laugh
     Gone !   and there is its cenotaph—
      Three grinning skulls !

V.

So passes all the year, and silently
    Beats the great heart of Nature in the earth,
Reneweth life, brings life to-day, yet she
    Travaileth naught to make the mighty birth :
So passes all the year, and jarringly
    Clash the small hearts of men, and grates each
      wheel
In the machine we call Society,
    While shrieks of death from their foul workshop
      peal :
So passes all the year, and gleefully
    Loves beast, and bird, and flower, each his kind :
The twittering lovers pair midst minstrelsy,
    The flowers' loves are wafted on the wind :
So passes all the year, and moodily
    Beats the fierce heart of man for woman's
      breast,
Love ploughs his soul as the storm-wind ploughs
      the sea,
    Lover and loved one tossed on its unrest.

VI.

Oh light, that smil'st at every cloud
  Flitting before the spring's glad breath ;
Oh light, my heart doth laugh aloud,
  Laughs at shadow and death.

Oh cloud, that laughest at the sun
  Rising out of the Eastern sea ;
Oh cloud, my shadow life is done,
  My light smileth on me.

Oh light, thy smile is dead—is dead,
  And the soft breeze hath sighed her last ;
Oh light, my smile of light is fled,
  My Heaven is overcast.

Oh cloud, that laughedst at the dawn,
  Midday frowns on the darkened main ;
Oh cloud, my laughless heart doth mourn,
  My sky melteth in rain.

Oh light, oh love born in her eyes,
  Oh cloud, oh heart that drank their light
Oh love, oh light, oh wintry skies,
  Veiling the tearful night !

VII.

Night, night - all through the cold, cold night.
Ah, woe is me !
All alone in the night ;
And the sleet drives down the Northern blast
Fast, fast,
Pours down the blast,
And the gloomy river creeps to the sea
Drearily.

Grave, grave — there is a cold, cold grave
Waiting for me,
All alone in the grave :
And thou wilt pluck a flower from the grass ?
Pass, pass,
Touch not the grass,
The worms beneath are waiting for thee
Hungrily.

Oh black sky, black river,
Wind that moan'st in the forest's gloom,
Billows of wintry ocean, whose boom
Maketh the cliffs that foil ye quiver.
Shall I be cold as now, shall I shiver
Sleeping there in the tomb ?

.   Light,
      God, there is light !
      One starry glance
Some angel has shed to break my trance.
Star, tell me, when was thy birth ?
    How many myriad ages thy beam
Has travelled to reach our rotting earth ?
    Yet fresh as a maiden's summer dream
    Of love is thy forget me not gleam.
So old, yet young   while our sodden earth
Rots in the very hour of her birth.
Oh, tell me, is there a future for me?
      Shall I live in death,
Or die while I draw my poisoned breath ?
    Must I too pass through the reeking soil
Into filth and impurity ?
    Must my dispersed particles toil
Into some slimy fungoid thing
In the dank shadow cowering ?
Or, shall I pass with meteor flight,
    Cleaving the void abyss,
    Into thy azure dream of bliss,
Into thy Heaven of Light?

                L

VIII.

Oh, sing, birds, sing in the merry trees,
Oh, ring bells, ring through the wind swept sky.
Oh, dance, wave, dance to the laughing breeze,
Dance to its melody!

Laugh flowers at the brook below,
Laugh at the smiling sun above,
Laugh at the shadows that come and go,
My heart is laughing with love!

Kiss her, breeze, as thou fleetest by,
Fresh is she as thy breath, oh spring.
Laugh, sun, in her melting eye,
My heart doth laugh and sing.

Myriad voices of all the Earth,
Lights of the empyrean dome,
Pour your sweetness in streams of mirth,
Smile and sing round her home.

Oh, sing, birds, sing in the merry trees.
A laugh in my heart and a smile in her eye,
Oh, ring, bells, ring down the laughing breeze,
Peal to the wind-swept sky.

ECSTASY.

Oh Sun, who smil'st abroad upon the sea,
Smile, smile upon my love, my love, and me:
Go to—thou laughest all too shamelessly,
    I blush in thy wanton light.

Oh Moon, who tremblest down the woodland stream,
Dost tremble at the beauty of our dream?
Fie, thou pale trembler!—hide thy quivering beam
    In the dark lap of night.

Oh Star, whose azure deeps of infinite rest
Smile down from Heaven, shed peace into my breast!
Nay, pass, cold orb, behind yon mountain's crest,
    Thou know'st nor smiles, nor sighs.

Oh Light, that light'st my soul's veiled sanctuary,
Oh Sun and Moon and myriad galaxy,
One Light, one Life, in all your moods to me,
    Light of two loving eyes!

EPIMETHEUS.

Wilt thou wouldst bid me stretch my little wings,
Into the poet's dreamland feebly soaring,
The True, the Good, the Beautiful adoring,
Sweep with my treble hand eternal strings,
The solemn music of eternal things

Wave upon wave upon the dull earth pouring
In thunder, till the echo of its roaring
Loud through the wide spread empyrean rings
Nay, sweet, no verse may scale my heavenly height,
Or pluck a star from out the void above

To awe men's souls to worship Tis thy kiss
Sends the warm rhythm dancing on its flight,
Its feet beat to thy heart beats, and thy eyes
Flash on my words and make them melodies